FLIPPER'S BOY

Designed by Bill Foster of Albarella & Associates, Inc.

Distributed to schools and libraries
in the United States by
ENCYCLOPAEDIA BRITANNICA EDUCATIONAL CORP
310 South Michigan Ave.
Chicago, Illinois 60604

Library of Congress Cataloging-in-Publication Data
Cebulash, Mel.
Flipper's boy / Mel Cebulash.
p. cm.
Summary: Tommy enjoys being a starter on his high
school basketball team, but he doesn't enjoy being
compared to the father who had deserted the family
when Tommy was very young.
ISBN 0-89565-881-X
[1. Basketball — Fiction.   2. Fathers and sons —
Fiction.]   I. Title.
PZ7.C2997Fl   1992
[Fic]—dc20   91-46504
                                                   CIP
                                                   AC

Sports

FLIPPER'S BOY

Mel Cebulash

Illustrated by:

Duane Krych

THE CHILD'S WORLD

ommy Mandell
figured the nervousness in his
stomach would disappear as
soon as the referee tossed up the
ball and the game started. Still,
Tommy didn't like the feeling.
He wasn't supposed to feel sick
about being in the starting lineup

of the Millersville High School basketball team. He was supposed to feel good.

Seconds later, Leon Hawkes tipped the opening tossup over to Tommy, and the hometown crowd of students and parents cheered enthusiastically. Tommy quickly dribbled toward his basket, while his teammates hustled into their offensive posts. He didn't have time to think about it, but his stomach no longer bothered him.

With a slight head fake and a burst of speed, Tommy got a step in front of the player guarding him and drove for the basket. Another player moved to keep Tommy from scoring, and Tommy immediately passed off to Ron Bittman. Ron's short jump shot went in clean and gave Millersville a 2–0 lead over West Washington High.

By half time, Millersville's lead had grown to 38–30, and it appeared as if the school's opening game of the season was going to be a winning one. Bobby "Papa" Briggs, the coach of the Millersville Rams seemed pleased. "You're looking like a team now," he told the players gathered around him in the locker room, "so just keep working together in the second half. Real teams are hard to beat in high-school play."

When the Rams returned to the court and started taking their mid-game practice shots, Tommy glanced over at the West Washington team and decided that they weren't thinking about losing. They looked determined and proved it by evening the score at 40-40 a few minutes after the second half started.

Then Papa Briggs signaled that he wanted the team to take

a timeout. "Settle down," he told
the Rams' starting five. "Those
boys scored some quick baskets
off you fellows, but they're not
playing team ball. Just be calm,
keep moving, and wait for your
shots. You'll win."

In the end, the Rams were up
by five points when the final
buzzer sounded. Leon Hawkes
topped the team scoring with
twenty-four points, while
Tommy contributed seven points
along with five assists. "Good
game, Leon," Tommy told the
tall center, as other players
slapped Leon's back and

congratulated him. "Hey," Leon said, looking slightly embarrassed, "we all played good."

"Yeah," Carlos Guerro joked, "I only missed all three shots I took. I'm going to have to shoot more."

"Is that right?" the coach said, surprising Carlos with his appearance.

"Just kidding, coach. I'll probably shoot less."

As soon as the coach left the locker room, Tommy and the others got on Carlos. "I'll never shoot again," Tommy joked.

"Hey, Coach," Fred Zeller said,

imitating Carlos, "could I be the team's designated non-shooter?"

By the time Tommy and the others were dressed and ready to leave the building, the grandstands were empty and the court lights were shut off. Outside, a few girls waited to meet players. One of them was Judy Roldino. Tommy was glad to see her. "I wasn't sure you'd be here," he said, glancing at his watch.

"I didn't want to walk home alone," she said, smiling as he took her hand. "By the way, you played a great game."

"I was all right, but Leon

played like a pro. He can probably pick the college he wants to attend."

"You can, too."

"Sure," Tommy said, laughing, "but let's get serious now."

They were still talking and joking when they reached Judy's front door. The lights were on inside the house. "Want to come in?" she asked.

"No, thanks. I don't feel like telling your father about the game and then having to go home and tell my mother the same thing. It gets boring."

"Okay, I'll see you in school."

Tommy kissed her quickly, wondering if her parents could see them through the lighted living-room windows. Then he turned away. "Hey," Judy called after him just as he reached the bottom porch step, "some guy in the stands yelled something about Flipper's boy just after you scored one of your baskets. Are you going to have to listen to stuff like that all season long?"

"Let's talk about it some other time," Tommy said, thinking Judy's father probably knew more about Flipper than he did. "My mother is waiting."

Tommy's mother had been home from work only a few minutes when he arrived. She was a waitress at the Millersville Diner and had heard that the Rams had won, but she wanted more details, especially about how Tommy had played.

When Tommy finished telling her about the game, she said, "It sounds as if you played fine. A lot of my regular customers were at the game, so they'll give me their opinions tomorrow night."

Tommy didn't say anything about the remark Judy had heard. His father, Roger "Flipper" Mandell, had been a popular basketball star at Millersville High. He and Tommy's mother had dated all through high school and married the summer after they'd graduated. Tommy had been born the following year.

Two years later, Tommy's

father had left — had moved
west, leaving his wife and
Tommy behind in Millersville.
Tommy hadn't seen his father
since then and really didn't
remember him at all. He'd
remarried and had a new family.
From what Tommy could tell,
he'd sent a check every once in
awhile for support, but that was
about it.

Barbara Mandell, Tommy's
mother, worked hard and put in
many hours. Still she never
complained about Tommy's
father. She even tried to tell
Tommy some stories about him,

but Tommy refused to listen to
them. His father didn't care
about him — that was obvious
enough. But Tommy wasn't
going to let that bother him.
He wasn't the first kid in the
world who had to grow up
without a father.

Tommy hadn't even heard his
father's nickname until he started
playing basketball on the junior-
high team. Then his mother told
him about Flipper because she
was sure people would ask him
about his father or start telling
stories about him. She was right.

Instead of listening to what

people had to say, Tommy cut them off by saying he hadn't seen his father since he was a little boy. He'd embarrassed some people by doing that and disappointed others who really just wanted to talk. Tommy didn't care. His father sure wasn't listening to any stories about Tommy, and Tommy didn't want to listen to any stories about his father.

In bed that night, Tommy recalled the conversation he'd had with the coach about a week after he'd tried out for the Rams. "I've been told that you

don't like to talk about your
Dad," Coach Briggs had said,
"and I respect that, but I need
to ask you a question, if you
don't mind?"

"No, I guess not."

"Did your father ever coach you?"

"No way!"

The coach had shaken his
head and looked puzzled. "Well,
Son," he'd said, "I won't say
another word about this, but you
move around the court and shoot
just like he did. It's amazing."

Tommy hadn't responded to
the coach's last remark, but "no
way" had been the words he'd

mumbled to himself. Playing like Michael Jordan interested Tommy. Playing like Flipper Mandell didn't. After that conversation the coach had kept his word, never mentioning Tommy's father and probably warning others not to mention the former Rams' star either.

Now Tommy was a starting player on the team. More people would see and hear his name. If they didn't know, they'd guess he was related to Flipper Mandell. After all, if the phone book was right, Tommy and his mother were the only Mandells in Millersville.

Tommy finally fell off to sleep. He was too tired to do any more thinking about Flipper Mandell. He really didn't care about him, and he certainly never expected to be reading about him in the newspaper the next morning.

When the alarm on Tommy's clock-radio sounded the next morning, he was almost glad to hear it. He was anxious to get the morning newspaper to see the story and box score of the game.

Tommy jumped out of bed

and quietly went to the front
door, trying hard not to disturb
his mother. Working the night
shift at the diner wasn't easy,
and she needed her rest. Still he
knew she'd get up if she heard
him. That was the way she was.

Opening the door slightly,
Tommy smiled as he caught
sight of the paper in the grass
about ten steps away. The kid
who delivered papers had either
a terrible arm or eye. Standing
there in his shorts, Tommy
momentarily thought of going
back to his room and getting his
bathrobe — something his

mother would have told him to do. Instead, he looked up and down the street. Then he raced for the paper and had it back in the house before anyone could get a good look at him.

Tommy rolled the rubber band off the paper and climbed back into bed, propping his back against the wall. He placed the first section of the paper by his side and focused his eyes on the first of several sports pages. The game was the feature story, and, as Tommy had imagined, the headline heralded Leon Hawkes' high-scoring effort. Tommy's eyes dropped to the box score. His name was spelled right, and the points he had scored were correctly recorded. Then he turned back to the story of the game and started reading it carefully.

Dan Seats, the sportswriter for the Millersville paper, always tagged his stories with a short section he called *From the Side Seats.* There Tommy spotted his name:

> For a few moments last night, it seemed as if the clock had been turned back almost 20 years. Tommy Mandell made some moves which seemed

like carbon copies of those made by Flipper Mandell back when he was starring for the Rams. Flipper hasn't been seen around here in years, but his son brings back fond memories of the great guard. Be nice to see old Flipper again, but if that can't be, let's hope that Tommy is the new Flipper.

Tommy crumpled the page and tossed it onto the floor alongside his bed. What was Dan Seats talking about? Why should Tommy have any interest in being the new Flipper? He didn't even have any interest in the old one.

Then Tommy climbed off the bed and tried to straighten the crumpled page. He did the best he could, but it still looked quite wrinkled. His mother would be sure to guess he hadn't liked what he'd read. He was going to have to get control of his temper, especially now because he was going to hear the name Flipper all day long. Maybe all season long.

Before placing the paper on the kitchen table for his mother, Tommy read Dan Seats' short column again. Tommy still didn't

like it, but he realized there was
nothing he could do about it. At
least, his father had been a
basketball star. Tommy tried to
imagine how he would feel if
his father had been a criminal,
but he wasn't sure he'd feel
any worse.

In school that day, Tommy
noticed none of his friends
mentioned the newspaper story.
Other kids who were unaware of
his nonexistent relationship with
his father, asked questions or
made remarks about the
nickname. Tommy pushed them
off by saying he didn't even

remember the man, and, to his surprise, most of the kids apologized for raising the subject.

The kids who bothered him were the ones who'd decided they liked the nickname. "Hey, Flipper," they called to him in a friendly way, as he walked through the halls. He tried not to answer, pretending he didn't recognize the name or hadn't heard it. Maybe it would soon be forgotten, but Tommy had his doubts about that by the end of the school day. He hoped practice wasn't going to be more of the same.

"Here's Flipper!" Leon Hawkes jokingly announced when Tommy stepped into the locker room.

"Hey," Papa Briggs called out before Tommy could respond, "we're going to have none of that Flipper stuff around here. It was a bad nickname when Tommy's father had it, and it sounds worse now. Tommy doesn't need any old, second-hand nicknames, so cool it. And if some of you can't cool it, I may have to make up some nicknames for you and pass them on to old Dan Seats. Now let's get dressed and get out there. We have a game on Friday."

As the coach passed Tommy, he winked. Tommy nodded in appreciation, but his mind was on something the coach had once said about moving around the court and shooting like his father. Tommy guessed he was going to be hearing that from a lot more people, unless, of course, they didn't see him that way. He got out of his street clothes as fast as he could. He was going to need a lot of practice.

"I went to all of your father's games," Tommy's mother told him that night, "but I don't remember them. It was a long time ago. He had a good jump shot. I do remember people saying that, but what difference does it make? You look a little like your father, so people probably go by that and say you play like him. Well, you play like yourself, and you'd better keep at it."

"Mom, why didn't Dad go to college if he was so good?"

Barbara Mandell smiled at the question. "That's one of the stories I wanted to tell you years ago," she said. "I guess Dan Seats' column did you some good. At least, it got you a little curious. Anyway, your father didn't like school. His grades weren't bad, but he was always restless in class. No one could

talk him into going to college.
Later, when we got married,
some people in town were
supposed to have said he didn't
go to college because I talked
him into getting married. I don't
think that idea got around very
much. I never heard any more
about it and never met anyone
who had. By the way, I think
your father had offers from over
twenty colleges."

"What does he do now?"

"Last I heard he was driving a
truck. I don't keep track of him,
but I do keep track of you and
you look tired. Go get some

sleep and quit worrying. You need to concentrate on the game Friday night. My customers tell me that Samson High has a strong team."

Tommy laughed. "Mom," he said, "you fall for some of the oldest jokes around. Samson — strong! Get it?"

"Oh, I heard the joke years ago, but isn't Samson supposed to be good this year?"

"Not good enough," Tommy boasted — but he wasn't as confident as he sounded.

Two nights later, Tommy realized why he hadn't been

confident. The Samson High team practicing at the other end of the court seemed to be moving smoothly, and even though many students and parents had come on school buses from Millersville to see the game, the cheering Samson fans gave their home team a big boost.

Tommy had another reason for lacking confidence. The driving hook shot he'd been practicing to replace his jump shot wasn't as easy to master as he'd hoped. Oh, it went in every now and then, but not enough to call it a good shot. Not enough, really, to call it a fair shot. Still the coach hadn't complained about it, so maybe it was better than Tommy thought.

Leon Hawkes tipped the opening tossup into Tommy's hands, as he'd done in their first game. Instead of waiting for his teammates to get into position, Tommy started dribbling upcourt, hoping to get a step ahead of the guy guarding him and either score a basket or draw a quick foul. Instead, Tommy had the ball slapped out of his hands, and by the time he stopped, turned and took off

after his man, it was too late.
Tommy's opponent was high in
the air and slamming home the
first points of the game.

Tommy missed two shots
before the guy guarding him
stole the ball again and shook
loose for another easy basket.
The Rams were down by seven
points, and the timeout Tommy
expected was called.

"What are you guys doing out
there?" Papa Briggs asked the
team, but his eyes were locked
on Tommy.

No one answered, so the
coach told them to slow the play

and work the ball into Leon as much as possible. "And Tommy," he said, "don't let that guy covering you run you off the court. He isn't as good as you're making him look."

Tommy felt the blood rushing to his face. "I'll try harder," he replied.

"Good," the coach said, slapping his back. "Now get out there and play like a team."

For the next few minutes, the Rams looked as if they were going to take control of the game. Leon scored eight points, and two of the baskets followed passes from Tommy.

Then the Samson players fought back and regained the lead on a beautiful, twisting jump shot by their center, following a bounce pass from Tommy's man. It was the same kind of pass the coach had been warning the Rams about all week long. Seconds later, Phil Gallagher rushed into the game, subbing for Tommy.

Off-court, Papa Briggs called Tommy to his side. "Let's give Phil a chance," the coach said. "This isn't your night."

Tommy settled down on the

far end of the bench. Judy was
in the stands, probably waiting
for him to look her way, but
he couldn't do it. He felt
too embarrassed.

He fixed his eyes on the court
and tried to concentrate on the
game. The Rams were racing up
and down the court, but
everything seemed blurry. The
coach's words echoed in
Tommy's ears. He didn't want to
believe them because they
meant he wouldn't get back into
the game again.

Samson High won the game by nine points. It was a bad loss for the Rams, but they were scheduled to play Samson again on Thursday in Millersville. "We'll even the score next week," Coach Briggs told them as they were dressing after the game. "So don't look so sad, and have a nice weekend. You'll lose other games in your life. I sure have."

Tommy understood what the coach meant, but he wasn't cheered by the idea. He'd been pulled out of the game early on and hadn't played another minute. Phil Gallagher hadn't played well either, but the coach had left him in the game. Tommy didn't want to think about that, but he couldn't help it. He wondered if he'd lost his spot on the starting team.

Judy was waiting for him in

the parking lot, and they quickly boarded one of the school buses. As they walked up the aisle toward one of the rear rows, a few students cheerfully remarked that they'd beat Samson next week, but the rest of the students and parents on the bus were either quiet or whispering to themselves. "We'd be singing and cheering if we'd won," Tommy remarked sadly.

"We might have won," Judy said angrily, "if the coach had given you a chance. You would have scored nine points. Phil Gallagher scored nothing."

"Thanks for being on my side," Tommy said, "but I wasn't exactly red-hot when I got benched. Didn't you notice?"

"You seemed to be a little awkward. Not like your old self, but I figured that was because of all the Flipper stuff you heard all week. My father said he didn't think it was going to be easy for you to be forced into the role of son of one of the greatest basketball players in the history of the Rams. I guess that stuff did make you nervous."

"Not really. The coach said it wasn't my night. Maybe that's all

it was. If I get to play again, I'll
find out."

Judy gasped. "Are you
kidding?" she said. "Do you
really think Phil will start against
Samson on Thursday?"

"I don't know what to think."

They rode on in silence.
When the bus got close to the
parking lot at Millersville High,
Judy said, "My father is probably
waiting for me. Want a ride home?"

"I'd rather walk," Tommy said,
"but I don't want him to think
I'm a sore loser or something
like that."

"He'll understand."

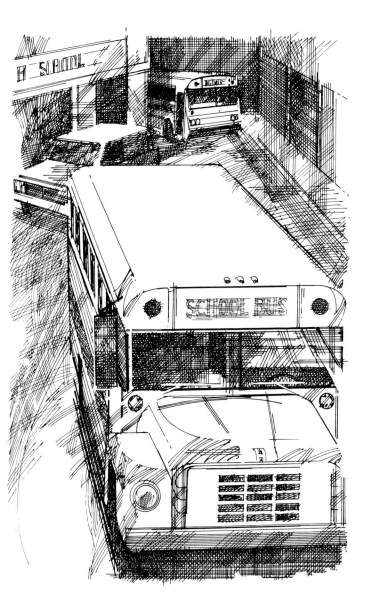

Barbara Mandell was sitting at the kitchen table when Tommy walked into the house. "I heard," she said sympathetically. "I gather it wasn't your night."

"That's exactly what the coach said when he took me out of the game. I guess the terrible way I was playing was obvious to everybody."

"I was talking with one of my customers about the game. I heard you were benched, but the man who told me didn't make any comments, except to assure me that you weren't injured."

"No, but I was worse than

terrible," Tommy said. "I don't even know if I'll be starting the next game."

"You probably will," Mrs. Mandell said, sounding as if she wanted to cheer him. "Coach Briggs is fair, so he'll probably give you another chance."

"I'll probably find out at practice on Monday. Well, I'm going to bed."

"Okay, go on, but quit looking so sad. There's a bright side to everything."

"Yeah, what's the bright side to this?"

"Dan Seats may never

mention your father again in
his column, and if he does,
he probably won't be
comparing you."

Tommy went off to his room.
He hadn't liked being compared
with his father, but now he
wasn't so sure he liked the idea
of not being compared with him
either. How good had his father
really been? And why was he
invading Tommy's life now,
when Tommy didn't want him in
it? Tommy fell asleep, wishing he
had answers instead of questions.

Before practice on Monday,
Coach Briggs answered one of

Tommy's questions. "Let me guess what that puzzled look on your face means," he said, smiling slightly. "You were benched on Friday and now you're not sure if you're starting Thursday. Well, you are, so get into your sweats and get out there."

Tommy smiled appreciatively. "Thanks, Coach," he said. "I'm sure I'll do better on Thursday."

"Sure you will. Oh, say, there's one other thing. Keep practicing that new hook shot of yours. It needs work."

"To be honest, I was just

shooting it because…."

"Hold on! I just got through telling you to work on it. Do you want to coach or play?"

"Play."

"Good decision."

As the Rams dressed for practice, they joked about giving Samson a haircut on Thursday night. Tommy grinned and tried to join in the friendly team spirit, but his mind was on the coach's suggestion. He hoped the coach wasn't risking another game just to help him get over Dan Seats' column about Flipper. It was beginning to seem like old news.

When the Rams and Samson lined up for the start of the game on Thursday night, Tommy sensed the confidence in Jeff Polan, the player who had guarded him the previous game. As they shook hands, Polan grinned and said, "Good to see you again."

Tommy nodded and bit down on his mouthguard. He guessed he should grin back and show Polan he wasn't being psyched out, but Tommy was too tight for that. He was anxious for the game to start.

The cheering Millersville crowd quieted down when Samson won the opening jump and quickly scored on a pass from Tolan to the Samson center who faked Leon Hawkes out of position and dropped in an easy turnaround jumper.

Tommy evened the score with

a driving jumper of his own, and the grin which had seemed frozen on Tolan's face disappeared. Still he managed to come back with a driving layup, and drew a foul which he also scored. "Relax," the coach called, as Tommy got ready to pass the ball into play again.

Moving deliberately, Ron Bittman worked the ball into Fred Zeller who, in turn, hit Leon Hawkes with a fine pass, and the Rams had another two points.

The scoring remained about even for the rest of the first half, and Samson High went off the

court with a one-point lead.
"They look a little tired," Papa
Briggs told the Rams in the
locker room, "so let's speed up
the play in this half. If you have
a shot, take it."

"All of us?" Carlos Guerro
said jokingly, and several
players laughed.

"Yeah," the coach said,
smiling broadly, "but having the
ball isn't the same as having a
shot, Carlos. I've told you that
about a thousand times."

"Only nine hundred, coach.
I counted."

As Tommy and the others

returned to the court for their
practice shots, he reviewed his
play. He'd scored five points and
contributed two assists. Polan
had seven points and a like
number of assists, but so far
Polan hadn't been able to steal
the ball from Tommy. He'd
blocked a jump shot though, and
Tommy hadn't been able to
block any of his shots. So their
play was close, and maybe that
was the reason the game was
close. Reason or not, Tommy
knew he had to do better. Close
didn't win basketball games.

The fast-breaking play the

coach had told Tommy and the others to use pushed them into a six-point lead soon after the second half started. Then, after a timeout, the Samson five seemed stronger. They slowed the pace of the game and chipped away the Rams' lead. With less than a minute left in the game, a bounce pass from Polan followed by another turnaround jumper from the Samson center put the score at dead even. The Rams quickly assembled around Coach Briggs for what was probably their last timeout.

"They're going to be

expecting a pass to Leon," the coach said, fixing his eyes on Tommy. "You dribble around and try to get it to Leon, but don't force the play. If it looks as if time is running out, you take the last shot. Take the hook shot."

"The hook shot?" Tommy said increduously. "I'm not very good at ...."

"Shoot it if time is running out. The worst that can happen is we go into overtime. Or are you guys too tired for overtime?"

"No," the Rams replied in unison, and they went back out onto the court.

As play resumed, Tommy shook off Polan and took the in-bounds pass from Ron Bittman. Tommy quickly dribbled toward Leon who had taken his place in the low post. Then reversing somewhat, Tommy tried to dribble to the side of Leon and pull his man off him momentarily. But the other center was glued to Leon, and Polan was beginning to glue himself to Tommy. Meanwhile, the clock was running out.

Tommy hated to shoot the hook. What did the coach have in mind, anyway? There wasn't

time for that. Tommy backed
toward the basket and threw a
shoulder feint. Polan went up to
block Tommy's jumper and was
on his way down when Tommy
let go of his hook shot. The ball
bounced off the backboard, hit
the rim, and fell back in as the
buzzer sounded.

The game was over. Tommy
had scored the winning basket.
The Millersville fans exploded
out onto the court. Tommy's
teammates hoisted him onto
their shoulders and carried
him through the crowd and off
the court.

Tommy was overjoyed because they'd won, but he also felt embarrassed. He'd made a lucky shot. He knew it, and he expected everybody else knew it, too.

The celebration continued in the locker room. When it died down, the coach called Tommy over to the side. "Good work," he said, giving Tommy a congratulatory backslap.

"Yeah, but it was a lucky shot. Didn't you see the way it bounced off the rim?"

"Right, it bounced in. It was good luck — and if it had

bounced out, it would have been bad luck. Sometimes I think life is nothing more than good and bad bounces, but the trick is to learn to live with the bounces. I told you to shoot — so, the way I look at it, I'm smart and you're lucky. Or we're both lucky. Anyway, enjoy the victory. We're going to have a lot of other hard games to play."

"Coach," Tommy said, as Papa Briggs started to move away, "why'd you tell me to shoot the hook shot? Just for luck?"

"No, I wanted you to get a shot, even if it wasn't your best —

and I was afraid the Polan boy
might block your jump shot if
you tried that."

"Hey, Hook Man," Leon called
from the other side of the room,
"come on over and show us how
you shot that."

Tommy looked at the coach.
"Go on, Hook Man," Papa Briggs
said, smiling at him.

As Tommy crossed the locker
room, he realized that he'd
probably gotten a new nickname
along with the winning basket. It
was his night.

Still, Tommy would always
be Flipper's boy in some way,

even if no one ever mentioned
it again. That was one of
the bounces.